Nicola Davies
A Boy's Best Friend

A Boy's Best Friend

Granny had given Clinton money to buy a soda at the Delroy Stores. He chose an orange crush, just like always, and, just like always, Mr Deroy leant over the counter to say hello to Clinton's companion.

'Good morning, Rufus, how are you today?'

Rufus wagged his tail, like a caramel coloured flag. Mr Delroy laughed.

'That dog is the best friend a boy could have.'

It was what everybody always said about Rufus. Cordel Anderson had said it that very morning when Clinton and Rufus had herded Granny's cows past his door. Aunty Sugar had said it yesterday while she leaned over the fence to watch Rufus help Clinton dig the garden. Most of all, Granny said it, and she had known Rufus for longer than anyone, since he was nothing but a ball of coffee-coloured fluff. Rufus was a grown up dog by the time Clinton came along, but that had never got in the way of their friendship.

'When your mum went to England,' Granny was fond of telling Clinton, 'that dog, he just stepped up to the plate to care for you!'

Clinton didn't know what sort of plate Granny was talking about, or why a dog would step up to it, all he knew was that Rufus understood him like no one else. Rufus knew when he was happy and they would run along the beach together; he understood when Clinton was sad and would lean against the boy's legs with a big, sympathetic sigh.

Mr Delroy handed Clinton an iced bun over the counter.

'Here,' he said, 'extra breakfast for you and your friend!'

Clinton thanked Mr Delroy; the bun was yesterday's, a bit stale, but still a kind thought. Clinton shared it with Rufus as they sat in the shade of the jacaranda tree and waited for the school bus. The sound of the waves shushed up from Souffay Beach and Clinton could see Mrs Edison and her sister unrolling their net. They'd need at least three other people to walk it out into the bay to catch fish. Clinton was thinking how much more he'd like to spend the day doing that than going to school when the bus arrived and swallowed him up. As usual, Rufus waited until the doors had swished shut before trotting off on his own business. It was easy to tell from the many brown-gold pups around the island that Rufus had a lot of girlfriends to visit!

Clinton got through the day at school the way he always did, by simply trying to ignore it. He stared out of the window at the floating clouds and the wind shivering the fingers of the palm leaves. Teachers told him off for daydreaming, so he just stared a bit harder. In the playground, he drank his soda slowly, noticing its delicious orange tang on his tongue and ignoring the children who teased him and called him names.

School was a trial, but when the bus doors swished open again, Rufus was waiting and Clinton was free! Together, boy and dog ran down onto the beach. The net was neatly rolled up between the rocks and Mrs Edison was selling the last of her fish from a bright pink bucket. Rufus trotted after a a few crabs, but they moved a bit too quickly for the old dog these days. He returned to Clinton's side and they stood looking at the clouds and the palm trees, and the bright line where the ocean met the sky. Rufus swished his tail from side to side as if he knew tomorrow was a Saturday.

Uncle Cecil tapped on Clinton's bedroom door very early the next morning, before it was light.

'Wake up, boy!' he whispered.

But Clinton was already up and dressed. Saturday was his favourite day of the week: there was no school and he got to go out fishing in his uncle's boat.

Clinton stepped onto the verandah, where Uncle Cecil stood waiting. Rufus pushed his way out through the screen door and stood, swishing his tail and looking up at them.

'One Saturday, we're going to have to take him with us,' Uncle Cecil said.

Clinton bent down and looked into the dog's tawny eyes.

'He knows he can't come, Uncle Cecil,' he said, 'he knows he has to stay and help Granny get the cows in!'

The screen door creaked again and Granny came trundling out, wrapped in her dressing gown.

'That's right!' she scolded. 'Can't have all my family deserting me! Here,' she continued, 'you forgot your lunches!'

She thrust two sandwich boxes and a large bottle of iced tea into Clinton's hands.

'You take care of this food, that brother of mine can't be trusted with a thing.'

Cecil rolled his eyes.

'Truly, the only reason I am a fisherman is to get away from my big sister and her nagging!' Then he kissed granny's cheek.

'Never mind your sweet-talking' she scolded, 'you take care of my grandson! And you,' she said, turning to Clinton, 'take care of my little brother.'

'I will, Granny' Clinton laughed, 'if you take care of my dog.'

'Sounds like we have a deal all-round,' said Cecil, 'now, can we go fishing?'

Close to shore, the sea was as flat as a mirror. The last stars gazed down at their own reflections and the boat left a wake that Clinton could trace right across the bay and back to Souffay Beach. As they drew away from the land, the swells began to grow, as if the ocean was taking great, slow breaths to bring in the dawn.

They were making for a tiny raft of rope and tarpaulin called a FAD, anchored to the ocean floor five miles out. Small fish gathered there to shelter and bigger fish came to hunt them. Spotting the FAD in the early light in these big swells was tricky. Cecil checked the coordinates on the GPS.

'We're almost on it. Keep an eye out, Clinton!'

Clinton had been coming out in Uncle's boat since he could walk, so balancing on a tipping deck was easy. He stood in the bow and scanned the rolling blue in front of them.

'Got it!' he cried, and pointed to the line of yellow buoys that appeared and disappeared a little way in front of the boat.

'Get those lines ready!' Uncle Cecil said. 'I have a good feeling about today!'

They baited the hooks with tiny silver sprats that Cecil had caught the day before and threw them into the water, close to the buoys. Clinton could just make out the shape of the tarpaulins billowing under the surface and the flash of small fish darting about. Almost at once they began to get bites and grinned at each other as they hauled the lines in. The fish fought hard for their lives, leapt and struggled and kept struggling, even when they lay defeated in the bottom of the boat. They were Mahimahi, dolphin fish, yellow and blue, not big for their kind, but each one still large enough to make a good dinner for a family. Soon there were fifteen or twenty of them in the bottom of the boat. Cecil and Clinton baited another round of hooks and hauled in six more. But, as the sun rose up the sky, the fish stopped biting.

'Let's get these home and sell them before it gets too hot,' Cecil said. 'You take the helm, boy!'

Clinton grinned. He loved steering the boat, holding her on course even when the swells and current tried to push her another way. Soon he was lost in the rhythm of the swells, steering up one and down the next, keeping his eye always on the peak of the island, showing like a misty smudge to the East.

Uncle Cecil usually joked and chatted when they'd had a good catch, but today he sat in the bow, quietly. After a while, he cleared his throat as if there were words stuck in there somewhere and turned to look at Clinton, with a very serious expression on his face.

'What do you plan to do with your life, Clinton?' he asked.

It was such an unexpected question that Clinton almost

toppled over the stern in surprise. He had never thought about 'his life', only of 'today' and 'tomorrow' and perhaps 'Saturday'.

'I could fish with you, Uncle!' Clinton stuttered. 'And keep some more cows maybe.' He trailed off.

Uncle Cecil shook his head.

'You're growing up, Clinton,' he said. 'There's no future on this little island for a bright boy like you.'

They fell silent once more. Cecil turned his head to watch the sea and Clinton concentrated on steering. Little by little the land on the horizon rose up to greet them; their island home. Clinton looked at its shape, high and green, with wisps of mist trailing from its peaks. It was his world. How could he, how could anyone, think of being somewhere else? But that was just what his mother had done. She had left the island far behind and gone to find a new kind of future for herself in London.

'One day, Clinton,' she had said, 'I'll send for you, and you can come to London too!'

That had been almost five years ago. A part of him still missed her very much, but he had Granny, Uncle Cecil and Rufus instead, the green island and the blue sea; none of those could be found in London.

They sold the mahimahi at the fish market in town but kept

some fish for themselves and for Mrs Edison. She and her family helped haul the boat up the sand when they arrived back at Souffray Beach. Uncle chatted like normal and there were no more awkward questions, but when they got back to Granny's house, 'normal' had gone missing. The table was set out on the veranda with a fancy white cloth and table napkins. Granny was wearing her best frock, the one she wore when the bishop came to give a sermon in church. When Clinton asked who was coming to dinner, Granny shrugged and said, 'Oh, just us,' and sent him off to get washed.

There were good things about the strange atmosphere: okra and cornmeal to go with their grilled mahimahi and banana crunch cake for pudding. Uncle Cecil and Clinton had two helpings of everything and Rufus got a piece of cake all for himself. At the end of the meal, just as Clinton was wondering if he could ever eat anything ever again, he noticed that Uncle Cecil and Granny were exchanging strange looks. Rufus came and put his head on Clinton's knee and gave a faint whimper. Something was coming.

Granny started to clear her throat, in the same way that Cecil had earlier. She put on her glasses and drew a letter out of her pocket. It had a British stamp and postmark and Mum's writing on the envelope. What had happened? Mum was terrible at writing letters.

'So,' Granny began, 'Cedella, your mother, has written me a letter, Clinton.'

Well, Clinton thought, I can see that.

'And in it, she tells me all about their new house, and your little sister and Adrian, your step-dad.'

Granny was talking to him as if he was three, it was very odd. And now Cecil joined in.

'This thing is,' he said, 'Cedella, your mother...'

'Uncle Cecil,' Clinton interrupted, 'I know my mother's name is Cedella.'

'Yes, yes, of course you do, well, the thing is...' Cecil ran out of words. He and Granny sat frozen, staring at each other, and then, at last, Clinton knew what the letter had said.

He sprang to his feet so suddenly that Rufus gave a little 'ruff' of alarm.

'No! No! I'm not leaving here. I'm not going to London. I don't want to. I don't have to.'

He realised he was shouting; he never shouted. He threw his napkin onto the table and ran down the steps towards the beach, with Rufus close behind him.

It was dark, but the stars were out and a big white moon sailed in the sky, casting skinny blue shadows over the sand and making the foam of the waves glow like neon. Pale ghost crabs skittered around the beach, but apart from that it was deserted. Clinton plonked himself down on the

sand and, with a huge sigh, Rufus came and leant against him, warm and soft. Clinton felt just awful. He did miss his mother. He did want meet his little sister at last. But the thought of leaving the island behind was horrible. He buried his face in Rufus' side.

Uncle Cecil came. He sat down on the sand next to Clinton and put his arm around him.

'I don't want to leave,' Clinton said miserably. 'Why can't they all come and live here?'

'Your mum never was much for fishing,' Cecil said, 'and I don't think swanky lawyers like Adrian would be any good at bringing in the cows, do you?'

Clinton couldn't help laughing.

'But I like fishing and I like cows,' he said.

'Then one day you can come back. But first, see what the world has to offer.'

'Why don't you and Granny come?'

'Because we really like fishing and cows!'

Clinton laughed again though his tears.

'Can I take Rufus?'

'You know you can't.' Uncle Cecil ruffled his nephew's hair. 'He likes cows even more than you do. What would he do in London?'

'But aren't all step-fathers cruel?'

Uncle Cecil laughed.

'Ah! You think he's going to turn you into a frog or something?'

Clinton gave his uncle's arm a little punch for making fun of him.

'I'm sorry, Clinton. I think this Adrian is good man. And I think he really wants you to be part of their family. Why don't you just try?'

So, it was decided. Clinton was going to leave the island behind and become a Londoner.

There was a lot to do to get ready. Applying for a passport took two trips to town, to get the special little photographs done in a booth next to the post office, to fill in forms and stand in lines. It was very dull. Mum sent money for new clothes because Clinton would be arriving in London in the winter and he'd need to be warm the moment he got off the plane. He tried on the long trousers and the sweatshirt. His body felt as if it was in a prison.

'I'll be too hot!' he complained. Granny and Uncle Cecil looked at each other and laughed.

Everyone at school heard that he was leaving and going to England. Children came up to him in the playground to ask questions; why was he going? Where would he live? What would he do? Clinton hardly knew what to say.

The date of his departure grew closer and closer. One day,

when Clinton and Rufus got in from school, Clinton's new passport, with its blue cover and neat gold letters, was on the kitchen table and, next to it, his plane ticket. Clinton sat down at the table and stared at them. It was happening. He was going to leave everything he'd ever known. For the first time, it felt real.

Rufus laid his head on Clinton's lap and whimpered softly. Clinton stroked the silky head; he hadn't noticed it until now, but the fur around Rufus' eyes and nose was snowy white, his whole muzzle and both ears too looked as if they had been touched with frost.

'How old are you now, boy?' Clinton whispered, 'Twelve? Thirteen, I think.'

If it was true what Granny said, that each dog year was worth seven human years, that made Rufus at least ninety-one. He was an old, old dog.

'Rufus, I'm going away to England,' Clinton told him, 'and I can't take you, boy.'

Rufus lifted his nose and licked the tears off Clinton's cheek.

The last days flew by. Clinton had tea with distant cousins he never knew he had. Neighbours popped by at all hours to wish him luck or to ask him to look up some relative or friend who went to England long ago. Rufus found it bewildering. He stuck even more closely to Clinton's side than ever. Every time Granny repacked Clinton's case, Clinton wished that he could simply pack his dog instead. He would miss Granny and Uncle Cecil, but they understood what was happening. All Rufus would know was that his best friend had deserted him.

On the morning of his final day at school, Mr Delroy gave him two buns, fresh from the oven, so that Rufus could have a whole one to himself. They sat under the tree waiting for the bus as usual and ate them. Then Rufus did something he'd never done before. He jumped up and put his paws on Clinton's shoulders, and looked intently into the boy's face. The dogs eyes were brown and tawny, flecked with little specs of gold. Clinton felt that in them he could see all the times they'd spent together: the mornings bringing the cows down the track, the afternoons on the beach, days in Granny's veg garden, the long history of their friendship. Then Rufus dropped onto all fours and trotted off, even before the door of the bus had opened.

All day, while teachers who had told him off smiled at him and girls who had never spoken to him before gave him good luck cards, Clinton thought about Rufus, those brown and gold eyes looking into his, and of the toffee-coloured back retreating down the the road. What had his friend been trying to say?

When the bus doors swished open at the end of the day

Rufus was not there to greet him. Clinton waited for ten minutes, twenty, half an hour, but the dog did not appear. He called in Delroy's but no one had seen Rufus since the morning. He crossed the beach, but Mrs Edison hadn't seen him either.

Clinton ran all the way home. Cecil had just got back with some fresh fish for their last evening meal together and Granny was up to her elbows in cake making. Rufus was no where. Not in the patch of sunlight on the verandah, not in the garden under the grapefruit tree, not up in the field with the cows. Clinton searched everywhere, called until he had no voice. When Cecil made him come in for supper, he felt too upset and worried to eat any of the lovely dinner Granny had cooked. When they got up early to leave for the airport, there was still no sign of Rufus.

'That old dog knows how to take care of himself.' Granny said, 'Don't you worry.'

'He just didn't want to say goodbye!' Cecil added.

*

Adrian dropped Clinton off at the school gates on his way to work.

'Cheer up!' he said. 'It's nearly spring.'

His whole family were always telling Clinton to 'cheer up'. 'Cheer up, we're going bowling tomorrow', or 'cheer up, we're going to the movies', or 'cheer up, we'll go for a pizza

and ice cream'. Clinton knew they were trying to be kind, doing their best to help him settle down in his new home. They had taken him on a big wheel they called 'The Eye', high above the city, taken him to see a famous football team play, and they had visited the crown jewels. He had a lovely bedroom in Mum and Adrian's house and his little sister, Lilly, already adored him. Mum was happy to have him close and Adrian was kind and funny and trying hard to be his dad. Even school was OK. He even had a friend, Josh, who was obsessed with history, castles and battles and something called *Vikings*. Josh was easy to be friends with because he did all the talking for both of them.

Clinton knew that he should be enjoying his new life. Instead, he felt like a lightbulb that had been turned off, dark and blank and hollow. When he spoke to Granny and Uncle Cecil on the phone there was never any news about Rufus.

'I think we may never really know what happened to him,' Uncle Cecil told him sadly.

Clinton felt that Rufus was doubly lost to him. Sometimes he wished he could wipe all his memories away, because remembering hurt so much.

Clinton trudged across the playground to the main door. The cold didn't help. Was there another colour in London except grey?

'Look!' Josh bounced up to him as he put his coat in his locker. Josh was very bouncy.

'Look!' Josh insisted, and pushed a paper under Clinton's nose. It was a photocopied sheet about a school trip to somewhere called Kent. 'Students will have the opportunity to visit one of the most famous Castles in the UK', it said.

'We have to go!' Josh said.

'But it's this Friday, won't all the places be taken?' Clinton asked.

'Ah, that's where inside information counts!' Josh grinned. 'I happen to know that Markus Stephens and Greg Lomax have got chicken pox!'

'But it's very expensive,' Clinton said.

'Oh come on, your parents are loaded.'

Clinton looked at the paper again. In tiny print at the bottom of the page it said:

'There will also be an option to visit a working farm.'

His heart leapt.

'I'll ask my parents tonight.'

'Yesss!' said Josh.

The school minibus turned off the motorway and headed down smaller roads. Josh was going on about moats and siege engines but Clinton wasn't listening. Adrian had said that it was nearly spring and here, away from the concrete and buildings, you could see that it really was. Fields shone green in the thin sunlight, big yellow flowers nodded here and there on verges. When they came to a field full of cows, Clinton wanted to shout for joy, even though they were black and white and very different from Granny's.

The minibus parked in the castle car park and the children headed off, led by Mr Parry, the history teacher. Clinton let them go and hung back to speak to Mrs Singh.

'It said on the sheet there was a farm visit,' Clinton mentioned shyly.

'Oh, Clinton, you had to sign up for it in advance,' Mrs Singh said, 'no one did, so we took it off the itinerary.'

Clinton tuned out for the rest of the day: the walking through huge rooms that no one seemed to live in, the exhibition about a war with loud noises and videos of planes and bombs and explosions, the moat, dark and dismal. At last they got back on the minibus. Josh went to sit next to a boy called Frank, fed up with Clinton's lack of interest. Clinton sat at the front, near the teachers.

'The traffic will be bad on the main road,' Mr Parry was saying, 'I'll take us through the lanes.'

Clinton shut his eyes and dozed off as the the minibus turned this way and that through the small, winding roads.

A horrible screech of brakes woke him. The minibus was spinning round! Clinton's seatbelt bit into his shoulder as they left the road. Through the window, Clinton could see the side of a huge tanker lorry moving towards them in what seemed like slow motion. Then it hit, and the impact juddered though Clinton's bones. There was a huge *BOOM* and a wall of flame rolled over. The bus stopped with a crunch.

'Out, out, out!' Mr Parry was yelling. Children were screaming and Mrs Singh was wrestling with seatbelts and pulling people up and out of the bus. Blood was pouring down her face. They staggered outside into a swirl of smoke and the smell of petrol. The tanker was in flames and had made a massive hole through the hedge. The minibus was half in, half out of a ditch. Children stood or sat in a daze, while the teachers tried to check that everyone was alright. Clinton felt as if he was looking at the scene from outside his own body.

Then out of the smoke came an old man in a grubby jacket and wellington boots. He walked with a stick and was trying to hurry. 'I need help,' he cried, 'that explosion made my cows stampede. If they run onto the main road...'

Everyone stared at him, too dazed to take in what he said. But Clinton understood at once what he was asking. Suddenly, he felt clear-headed and alive.

'I'll help,' he said, 'I know about cows.'

Clinton set off through the smoke with the man. Mr

Parry yelled 'Come back!' but Clinton just tuned him out.

'I'm David!' said the man , 'and this is Tessie.'

A bright eyed, black and white dog ran beside them.

'I think we can head them off at the bottom of the next field,' David said, 'if you can help herd them up then close that gate behind them, then they can't get on the road.'

Clinton looked down the slope. A herd of twenty or so big brown cows, bellowing in fright, were tearing towards the lines of fast-moving traffic. If he and Tessie moved at David's hobbling pace, they would not make it.

'You wait at the gate, David,' Clinton said, 'me and Tessie will get in front of them and head them off.'

Clinton had only to say, 'C'mon Tessie,' and they were off.

If they came up behind the cows it would only make them run faster towards the road. Clinton could see they'd have to skirt around in the ploughed field next door, then get through the hedge at the bottom. It was quite a distance. He'd have to run faster than he had in months, but somehow having a dog running beside him made his feet fly.

They raced on. Just a shallow ditch now stood between them and the road where cars whizzed along, their lights glowing in the falling light. Clinton could hear the cows mooing and the sound of their hooves. He and Tessie would need to make a big effort to to get them to turn around. As they reached the end of the field, Clinton spotted a bright blue plastic sack caught in the hedge. He grabbed it and, with the dog at his heels, flew around the bottom edge of the hedge, where it ran into the ditch.

They were just in time. The cows were wild-eyed and running hard, moments away from the road. If they ran into the traffic, who knew what might happen. Clinton didn't hesitate. He jumped out into their path with Tessie. He shouted and waved the plastic sack and Tessie barked and snarled like a whole pack of wolves. The cows slid into each other, fell, got up, bellowed and fussed in a tangle, but they turned around. Then, because running up the steep hill when they were already out of breath was too hard, they slowed down and began to calm as they climbed back up the slope.

Tessie ran back and forth behind the herd, gently reminding them of the direction they were supposed to be going. At last, they went through the gate and David clanged it shut behind them.

David shook Clinton's hand and patted him on the shoulder.

'I can't thank you enough, lad,' he said. 'You did a fine job, saved my cattle and a few human lives, I'd say.'

'Thanks!' he said. 'I used to help every day with my Granny's cows.'

'Well it shows!' said David. Tessie nuzzled Clinton's hand.

'She's taken a shine to you!' David laughed.

They walked up the field and through another gate to the lane leading back to the minibus.

'That's my place,' said David, pointing to the the cottage opposite where they stood. There was a veg garden, neatly dug, with labels marking the rows of seeds that had been planted. Chickens clucked in a pen and the place smelled of cows. The only thing that was missing was Uncle Cecil's fishing gear and a grapefruit tree.

'It looks lovely,' Clinton said, 'reminds me of home, I mean, Granny's house.'

David looked into his face. 'You miss it, then?'

Clinton nodded.

'Come back and visit. You can help out on the farm. I could do with a helping hand.'

'Oh, yes please,' said Clinton, 'I'd love that.'

'You make sure you do!' David replied, 'Always good to meet a fellow farmer!'

They shook hands and Clinton ran up the lane, towards the blue lights.

Clinton was in a lot of trouble for running off after the accident. Everybody from his headteacher to his mum and Adrian had something to say about it. They called him 'irresponsible', 'reckless', 'inconsiderate'. Nobody wanted to hear about the stampeding cows and David's fall, or how he had felt standing in the vegetable garden with the chickens and the dog.

It was spring now, and even in the city there were bits of green. It stopped raining sometimes and the sun was sort of warm. On Sundays they went to the park so Lilly could play on the swings. Clinton loved watching her smile and squeal when he pushed her high. It seemed like Lilly was the only person left in the world who wasn't angry with him.

Then one morning, at half term, weeks after the school trip and the accident, a letter came with spidery handwriting. It was addressed to 'The Parents of Clinton' and had been sent to school first and readdressed. It was from David! His writing was wobbly and a bit hard to read, but it said everything that Clinton had been trying to explain and no one had wanted to hear: about the tanker burning a hole in the hedge, about the cows stampeding and nearly getting onto the main road, and about Clinton's prompt action had saved the day.

Adrian read out some of what David had written:

'Clinton showed great presence of mind, courage, and kindness. I do not like to think what would have happened that evening if Clinton had not been there to help. Many lives may have been lost.

'You must be very proud to have such a brave and capable son.'

'Oh Clinton,' Adrian said, 'I'm so, so sorry.'

Mum gave him a huge hug.

'Why didn't you tell us?'

Clinton didn't say that he had tried to.

'This gentleman has invited us to his farm,' Adrian said, waving the letter, 'I think we should go today!'

As they left the city behind, Clinton began to feel his heart lift. Lily looked out of the window and said,

'Cows!' or 'Baa lambs!' and did animal sound effects to make her brother laugh.

Most astonishing of all, Adrian told a story about how he loved to visit his great-aunt's farm in Wales.

'I used to love bringing the cows in from the fields,' he said.

When they got to Field's End Cottage, David was in his veg garden. He greeted them with a huge smile.

'What a lovely surprise!' he said. 'Let me show you round!'

David gave them a tour of the farm, the chickens, the veg garden and the brown cows grazing peacefully in the field above the main road.

'Your boy ran like the wind,' David said, 'stepped out and turned this herd around. They look calm enough now, but they were wild with fear!'

Mum squeezed Clinton's shoulder and Adrian wiped some dust out of his eye.

'A very fine lad you have here!' the old man added.

Lily loved feeding the chickens and Adrian turned out to be pretty good with a spade. Mum helped David with the weeding.

'I'd forgotten how much I liked this!' she grinned.

'Ah, be careful what you say,' David laughed, 'I'll have you doing this every weekend!'

'I don't think anyone would mind!' said Adrian.

It was funny to see Mum, Adrian and Lilly in jeans and muddy wellies, looking as happy as Clinton felt.

But there was somebody missing: Tessie. Where was she? Clinton was almost afraid to ask about her, in case she too had disappeared. At last, he decided he had to know.

'Where's Tessie?' he asked David quietly.

David grinned. 'Oh I'll show you.'

Clinton took Lilly's hand and they all followed David into one of the barns. A chorus of yips and whimpers greeted them. Jessie, followed by four sturdy pups, like little black and white bears, rushed out to greet them.

They were gorgeous! Clinton crouched down and let them snuffle round him. Lily giggled with delight, and Mum and Adrian cooed as if the pups were new human babies.

'Ah,' said David, 'here's the last!'

There was one more pup, a little bigger than the rest. He walked straight up to Clinton and boldly put his paws on the boy's knees. David laughed.

'Well,' he said, 'I was going to offer you the pick of the pups as a thank you present. But it looks like one of the pups has picked you!'

The pup wasn't black and white like the others. It was mostly brown, like caramel, splashed with white. Its eyes were brown and tawny with gold flecks. Clinton gazed into them and saw his past with his dear old friend Rufus;

beaches and palm trees, hummingbirds and verandahs, Granny and Uncle Cecil. But he saw, too, happy days to come: walks in the park, kicking leaves in the autumn, visits to David's farm, cosy afternoons snuggled by a fire. He saw his family, Mum and Lily, Adrian and himself, and their dog, his new best friend.

'Well,' said Adrian, 'I think we just got a new family member!'

'Will you call him Rufus?' asked Mum.

Clinton shook his head.

'No,' said Clinton. 'I'm going to call him London, 'cos that's where we all live.'

London licked Clinton's hand to say he approved of his new name, and Clinton felt the sunlight of the day shine right into his heart.

Nicola Davies

Nicola is an award-winning author whose many books for children include *The Promise* (Green Earth Book Award 2015, CILIP Kate Greenaway Medal Shortlist 2015), *Tiny* (AAAS/Subaru SB&F Prize 2015), *A First Book of Nature*, *Whale Boy* (Blue Peter Book Awards Shortlist 2014), and the Heroes of the Wild series (Portsmouth Book Award 2014).

She graduated in Zoology, studied whales and bats and then worked for the BBC Natural History Unit. Underlying all Nicola's writing is the belief that a relationship with nature is essential to every human being, and that now, more than ever, we need to renew that relationship.

Nicola's children's books from Graffeg include *Perfect* (2017 CILIP Kate Greenaway Medal Longlist), *The Pond* (2018 CILIP Kate Greenaway Medal Longlist), the Shadows and Light series, *The Word Bird, Animal Surprises* and *Into the Blue*.

Cathy Fisher

Cathy Fisher grew up with eight brothers and sisters, playing in the fields overlooking Bath.

She has been a teacher and practising artist all her life, living and working in the UK, Seychelles and Australia.

Art is Cathy's first language. As a young child she scribbled on the walls of her bedroom and ever since has felt a sense of urgency to paint and draw stories which she feels need to be heard and expressed.

Cathy's first published books with Graffeg include *Perfect*, followed by *The Pond*, written by Nicola Davies. Both books were Longlisted for the CILIP Kate Greenaway Medal.

Country Tales series by Nicola Davies

Flying Free
Nicola Davies
Illustrations by Cathy Fisher

The Little Mistake
Nicola Davies
Illustrations by Cathy Fisher

The Mountain Lamb
Nicola Davies
Illustrations by Cathy Fisher

A Boy's Best Friend
Nicola Davies
Illustrations by Cathy Fisher

Pretend Cows
Nicola Davies
Illustrations by Cathy Fisher

Spikes and Sam
Nicola Davies
Illustrations by Cathy Fisher

Visit our website author pages www.graffeg.com for more about
the author Nicola Davies and illustrator Cathy Fisher, plus a complete
list of our children's books and merchandise.

ZOMBIE WASPS

MIKE GOULD

Contents

MONSTER SPIDER...CRAWLING TERROR 100 FEET HIGH!

RESEARCHERS SEEKING CLUE!

CAN ANYTHING ESCAPE IT?

TARANTULA!

STARRING **JOHN AGAR · MARA CORDAY · LEO G. CARROLL**

Flesh-eating zombies? Giant creepy-crawlies?
Films are full of them.

But look out at your garden or by the side of
the road. There are monsters out there, too.
And lots of them are bugs.

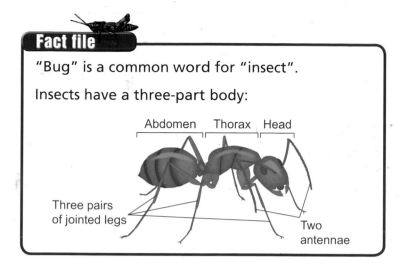

The Scare Scale

Of course, not everyone's scared. Where do

you fit on the Scare Scale?

Terrified

Very scared

Quite scared

Don't like them

OK

Not scared at all!

3

Scary stingers

Bees, ants and wasps are all insects that sting.

Asian giant hornet

Keep out of the way of this guy. In Japan, this bug kills more people than all other creatures put together. And that includes wild bears!

It is about 50 mm long and has a wingspan of 76 mm.

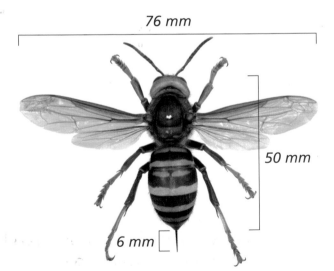

76 mm

50 mm

6 mm

Its stinger is about 6 mm long.

It is found in the parts of the world shown here in orange.

EUROPE

ASIA

AFRICA

INDIAN OCEAN

AUSTRALIA

Did you know?

Probably hundreds of people are killed each year by this bug. Honey bees are its favourite food.

Zombie wasps

Picture a zombie. A dead thing taken over by an evil force.

Then, check out that scene in the film *Alien*.

The one where the alien bursts out of someone's stomach.

That is what zombie wasps do to ladybirds, caterpillars and other creatures.

A female wasp injects its egg into the body of another insect, like a ladybird.

The **larva** hatches from the egg and eats the ladybird's insides.

Then it bursts out through the abdomen.

Venom from the mother wasp **paralyses** the ladybird. The ladybird twitches but can't move of its own accord.

> **larva** the stage of an insect's life after the egg
>
> **paralyses** makes it unable to move

Tarantula hawk wasp

This is a type of zombie wasp.

Its prey is the tarantula spider!

First, it grabs one
of the spider's legs with its jaws.

The spider tries to fight back, but the wasp
stings it until it stops moving.

Then, it drags the spider off to its nest and lays
an egg on it.

The wasp larva feeds inside the living spider,
before finally killing it weeks or months later.

Scientist Justin Schmidt made a scale to measure how bad stings are.

He found out by letting lots of different bugs sting or bite him!

Here are some examples:

Index 1.0   Sweat bee

Light, as if a tiny spark has singed a single hair on your arm.

Index 2.0   Honey bee

Stronger, like a match burning your skin.

Index 4.0   Tarantula hawk wasp

Bad, as if someone has dropped a hairdryer into your bath.

Giant bugs

Most people think bugs are small, but some of them are huge.

Hercules moth

The Hercules moth has a wingspan of up to 29 cm. That's about the same as the length of a piece of A4 paper.

Why is it called the Hercules moth?

Hercules was a huge half-god, half-human from Roman legend. He was incredibly big and strong, like the Hercules moth.

Titan longhorn beetle

This is another huge insect. It is the world's longest beetle, if you don't include the jaws and horns.

It can grow to nearly 17 cm long.

The male never feeds. It just searches for a mate!

If it is scared, it hisses at you. Its jaws are strong enough to snap a pencil in half.

Giant centipede

This monster is the world's biggest centipede.

Its maximum body length is 35 cm.

They like to attack, and they have a nasty bite.

Fact file

Found in: northern South America

Eats:

crickets
beetles
tarantulas
frogs
lizards
mice
birds

NORTH
AMERICA

EUROPE

ASIA

ATLANTIC
OCEAN

AFRICA

PACIFIC
OCEAN

SOUTH
AMERICA

INDIAN
OCEAN

*A pair of claws with **venom** (poison) inside*

Did you know?

They have been filmed in caves hanging upside down.

They were catching flying bats with their front eight pairs of legs!

13

Emperor scorpion

This is the world's biggest scorpion.

It is found in West Africa, and lives in burrows with up to 20 others. Yuk!

Its usual length is between 13 and 18 cm.

It doesn't sting much, but uses its giant claws to crush its prey, usually beetles and millipedes.

There are 1700 species of scorpion across the world. The one to avoid is the death stalker, which has a deadly sting. It is found in the deserts of North Africa and the Middle East.

A mother carrying its young on its back

How does an emperor scorpion catch its prey?

Step 1: **Waits** without moving in the mouth
of its burrow.

Step 2: **Watches** for
passing prey.

Step 3: **Rushes out** and
grabs the passer-by.

Step 4: **Drags it back** into the burrow
and eats it!

Special file: The Size Scale

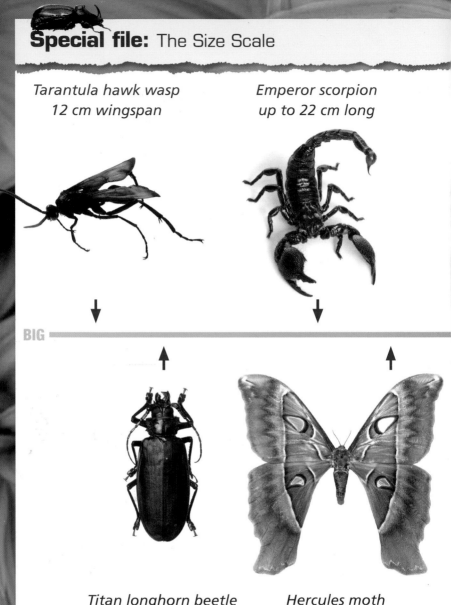

Tarantula hawk wasp
12 cm wingspan

Emperor scorpion
up to 22 cm long

BIG

Titan longhorn beetle
16 cm long

Hercules moth
29 cm wingspan

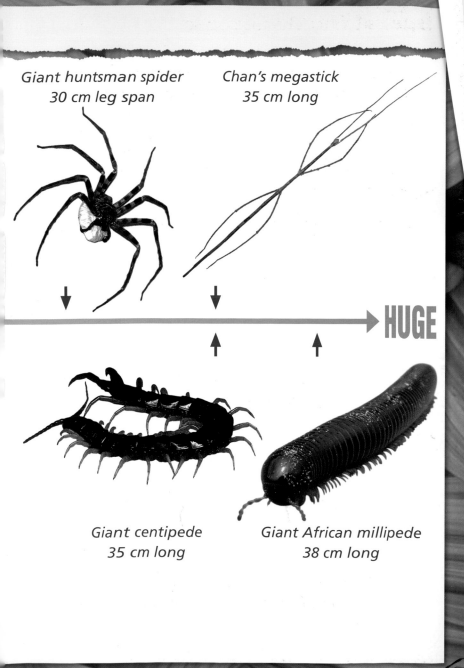

Giant huntsman spider
30 cm leg span

Chan's megastick
35 cm long

HUGE

Giant centipede
35 cm long

Giant African millipede
38 cm long

17

Armies, swarms and fighters

One nasty bug can be a problem.

But what about an army of thousands?

Ants

Ants work, live and fight together.

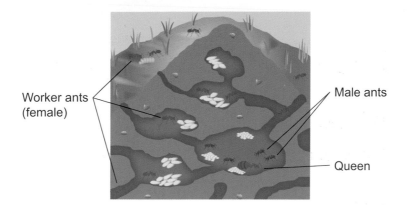

Worker ants (female)

Male ants

Queen

In an ant colony you will find:

the queen – her job is to lay eggs

male ants – they don't do much except mate and die!

worker ants – they are females and protect the queen, find food and fight off enemy ants from other colonies.

Did you know?

- Some of the worker ants are called soldier ants.
- Some soldier ants have heads shaped like the holes to their nest. They use their heads to stop enemies getting in.
- A few types of ant steal eggs from other colonies, then make slaves of them when they hatch!

The warlike termite

Warlike termites look similar to ants – apart from their nest. It is a big mound of earth with a shaft running up the centre.

The queen termite filled with eggs

Several million termites live in it. They are all the children of a single king and queen who live inside.

The queen lays about 30,000 eggs a day. That's 10 million each year.

Individual termites live about one year, but the king and queen may live up to 20 years or more. That's a lot of eggs.

Do the maths!

Did you know?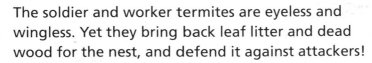

The soldier and worker termites are eyeless and wingless. Yet they bring back leaf litter and dead wood for the nest, and defend it against attackers!

The bullet ant

The bullet ant is one of the world's largest
ants. It's a real fighter.

It is number four in the Schmidt Sting Pain
Index (see page 9) and is found in Central and
South America.

If you're stung by one, it feels like you've
been shot!

Did you know?

They are sometimes called "24 hour ants" because it takes that long for the pain of a sting to wear off.

Africanised honey bee

This should be called the Frankenstein bee.

Dr Frankenstein created a monster by mixing different body parts together. It was an experiment that went wrong.

In the bee experiment, someone mated European honey bees with African bees. They wanted to create super bees that would make more honey. Unfortunately, some of the African bees escaped and mated with local bees.

The result? A bee that is quick to attack in huge swarms.

Why is it so dangerous?

When one stings you, it lets out a special banana-like smell. This tells other bees to attack. Hundreds can sting you at once.

These bees can swarm and attack a long way from their hive.

Did you know?

People still use them for producing honey!

Read all about it!

Bee swarm kills couple

19 April 2011

90 year old William Steele was spraying a bees' nest at his ranch in Texas when the bees started attacking him and his wife.

The swarm killed them both.

Mrs Steele was stung 300 times.

The bees also attacked their son and the police who arrived on the scene.

There have been films made about killer bees. Here are two well-known ones:

The Savage Bees (1976)

This one is about bees attacking people at a festival.

The Swarm (1978)

This is about killer bees invading Texas.

Hidden horrors

Some insects can be hard to spot. They use colour or shape to blend in with their background.

We call this **camouflage** – like the clothes soldiers often wear.

Insects do this to hide from their enemies. Or to ambush their prey.

Look at these pictures.

Can you see the insect in each one?

The brown recluse spider

If you are someone who likes to keep out of people's way, you might be called a **recluse**. That is how this spider got its name.

Just as well, as it has a bite that can kill.

This spider likes anywhere dry and warm, such as sheds, garages or cardboard boxes. However, it has been found in gloves, shoes and even piles of clothes!

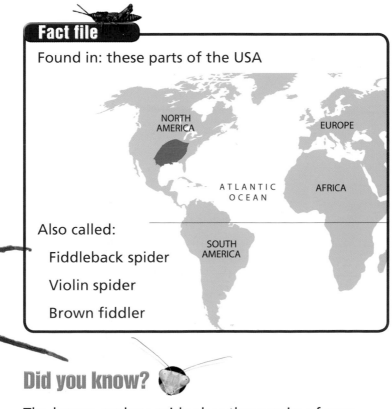

Fact file

Found in: these parts of the USA

NORTH AMERICA

EUROPE

ATLANTIC OCEAN

AFRICA

Also called:

SOUTH AMERICA

Fiddleback spider

Violin spider

Brown fiddler

Did you know?

The brown recluse spider has three pairs of eyes. Is that a sixth sense?!

Giant Asian mantis

Look at how close in colour this mantis is to the leaves around it.

You wouldn't want to be a passing mouse, tree frog or lizard. This mantis eats them all.

The females eat their male partners, too! They often attack, kill and eat males just after mating.

How romantic.

Found in: these parts of Asia

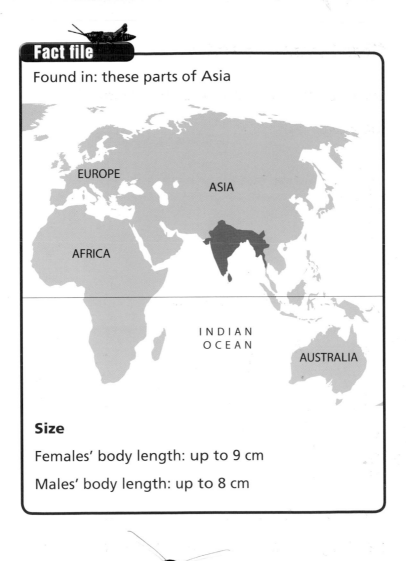

EUROPE

ASIA

AFRICA

INDIAN
OCEAN

AUSTRALIA

Size

Females' body length: up to 9 cm

Males' body length: up to 8 cm

Did you know?

They have large eyes and can turn their heads 180 degrees. While they do this, the rest of their body stays still.

It is said that kung-fu expert Wang Lang learnt some of his best moves from a mantis.

One day, in the woods near his temple, Wang saw a mantis fighting a bigger insect.

The mantis won by using its arms to "climb" its opponent.

Wang took the mantis back to the temple and spoke to it. "Maybe you can teach me something," he said.

He used a piece of straw to prod the mantis.
Then he watched how it attacked.

Wang developed new moves based on what
the mantis did.

When his master returned to the temple,
Wang beat him for the first time.

Together they developed a new form of
kung-fu. They called it "Mantis boxing".

Your worst bug

You have seen quite
a few beastly
insects in this book:

- big ones, like the
  giant centipede

- tiny terrors, like the bullet ant

- zombie-like monsters, like the tarantula
  hawk wasp.

What makes a bug *really* scary? Is it …

- how strong its poison is

- how big it is

- how clever and cunning
  it is?

What would be *your* scariest insect?

Perhaps it isn't in this book. Perhaps it hasn't even been found yet.

Go out into your garden or into a nearby field or wood. Lift up a branch, or look under some leaves or plants. Perhaps you will find a terrifying, flesh-eating monster bug …

Reader challenge

Word hunt

1 On page 14, find a verb that means "squash".

2 On page 20, find a noun that means "pile".

3 On page 28, find a noun made of two words.

Text sense

4 Why do some insects use camouflage? (page 28)

5 Where does the recluse spider like to live? (page 31)

6 What are the other names for the recluse spider? (page 31)

7 Why do you think the Giant Asian mantis turns its head right round? (page 33)

8 Do you think the story on pages 34 and 35 is true?

Your views

9. What would be your scariest insect?
Give reasons.

10. Did you enjoy reading *Zombie Wasps*?
Give reasons.

Spell it

With a partner, look at these words and then
cover them up.

- scare
- scale
- escape

Take it in turns to read the words aloud.
The other person has to try and spell each
word. Check your answers, then swap over.

Try it

With a partner, quickly look through the text
and find as many names of bugs as you can.
Play the memory game and take it in turns to
name one of the bugs. The first person to be
unable to think of an insect name is the loser.

William Collins's dream of knowledge for all began with the publication of his first book in 1819. A self-educated mill worker, he not only enriched millions of lives, but also founded a flourishing publishing house. Today, staying true to this spirit, Collins books are packed with inspiration, innovation and practical expertise. They place you at the centre of a world of possibility and give you exactly what you need to explore it.

Collins. Freedom to teach.

Published by Collins Education
An imprint of HarperCollins*Publishers*
77–85 Fulham Palace Road, Hammersmith, London W6 8JB
In association with the Natural History Museum.

Browse the complete Collins Education catalogue at **www.collinseducation.com**

Text by Mike Gould © HarperCollins Publishers Limited 2012
Based on the book *Big Bugs Life-size* by George Beccaloni © Natural History Museum, London, 2010

Series consultants: Alan Gibbons and Natalie Packer

10 9 8 7 6 5 4 3 2 1
ISBN 978-0-00-748476-8

British Library Cataloguing in Publication Data.
A catalogue record for this publication is available from the British Library.

Commissioned by Catherine Martin
Edited and project-managed by Sue Chapple
Picture research and proofreading by Grace Glendinning
Illustration management by Tim Satterthwaite
Design and typesetting by Jordan Publishing Design Limited
Cover design by Paul Manning

Acknowledgements

The publishers would like to thank the students and teachers of the following schools for their help in trialling the Read On series:

Southfields Academy, London
Queensbury School, Queensbury, Bradford
Langham C of E Primary School, Langham, Rutland
Ratton School, Eastbourne, East Sussex
Northfleet School for Girls, North Fleet, Kent
Westergate Community School, Chichester, West Sussex
Bottesford C of E Primary School, Bottesford, Nottinghamshire
Woodfield Academy, Redditch, Worcestershire
St Richard's Catholic College, Bexhill, East Sussex

The publishers gratefully acknowledge the permission granted to reproduce the copyright material in this book. While every effort has been made to trace and contact copyright holders, where this has not been possible the publishers will be pleased to make the necessary arrangements at the first opportunity.

The publisher would like to thank the following for permission to reproduce pictures in these pages (t = top, b = bottom, c = centre, l = left, r = right):

All pages: Jacob Hamblin/Shutterstock, pp 5, 13, 19, 21, 23, 25, 31, 33 hwongcc/Shutterstock, p 2c Pictorial Press Ltd/Alamy, p 2t fivespots/Shutterstock, p 3cr Artem Svystun/Shutterstock, p 3br Neo Edmund/Shutterstock, p 3cl Maridav/Shutterstock, p 3cr Maridav/Shutterstock, p 4t Biehler, Michael/Shutterstock, p 4b LAWRENCE LAWRY/SCIENCE PHOTO LIBRARY, p 6 William Attard McCarthy/Shutterstock, p 7 © Mathieu B. MORIN - IRBV 2012, p 8c Eric Isselée/Shutterstock, p 9 Scott Bauer, USDA Agricultural Research Service, Bugwood.org, p 10t Pan Xunbin/Shutterstock, p 10b Universal History Archive/Getty Images, p 13 Tim Green/BBC, pp 14–15 Dorling Kindersley/Getty Images, p 15 PASCAL GOETGHELUCK/SCIENCE PHOTO LIBRARY, p 16tr Eric Isselée/Shutterstock, p 16tl Brand X Pictures/Getty Images, p 17br Bjørn Christian Tørrissen/WikiMedia Commons, p 17bl INTERFOTO/Alamy, p 17tl Petra & Wilfried/WikiMedia Commons, p 18t Redmond O. Durrell/Alamy, p 18b PATRICK LANDMANN/SCIENCE PHOTO LIBRARY, p 20 Ed Reschke/Getty Images, p 21 wonderisland/Shutterstock, pp 22-23 Redmond O. Durrell/Alamy, p 23 Piotr Naskrecki/Getty Images, p 24t Photos 12/Alamy, p 24b KPA/Zuma/Rex Features, p 25 Daniel Plumer/Flickr, p 26 Peter Waters/Shutterstock, p 27b AF archive/Alamy, p 27t Photos 12/Alamy, p 28 photo by Spc. Kristina Gupton/The U.S. Army/Flickr, p 29b Piotr Naskrecki/Getty Images, p 29t Don DeBold/Flickr, pp 30–31 Florida Division of Plant Industry Archive, Florida Department of Agriculture and Consumer Services, Bugwood.org, p 32 Keith Poynton/Alamy, p 34 Tom Wang/Shutterstock, p 35 Eric Isselée/Shutterstock, pp 36–37 fivespots/Shutterstock.

The following images have been provided courtesy of the Natural History Museum, London:

p 8t, p 10c, p 11, pp 12–13, p 12b, p 16br, p 16bl, p 17tr, p 33 ©The Natural History Museum, London.